Scooby-Doo! You:
A Collect the Clues Mystery
THE CASE OF THE LOST LUMBERJACK

By Jesse McCann

WB WORLDWIDE PUBLISHING™

SCHOLASTIC INC.

New York Toronto London Auckland Sydney
Mexico City New Delhi Hong Kong

To Jesse Blake and
Amanda Teresa, my beloved
children. To you my heart, my
everything.

ISBN:0-439-21754-7

12 11   4 5/0

Cover and interior illustrations by Duendes del Sur
Cover and interior design by Madalina Stefan

Printed in the U.S.A.

First Scholastic printing, November 2000

On the way home, you notice a very different kind of van at the car repair garage. It's green, with cheerful designs and writing on the side. It's the Mystery Machine!

"Wow! There's something you don't see every day," you think to yourself.

But the Mystery Machine has been all taken apart and its owners are nowhere to be seen.

Where are Scooby-Doo and the other members of Mystery, Inc.?

Then you hear a familiar voice.

"Hey, friend! We're over here!" It's Velma, calling to you.

You turn and look.

Sure enough, there's the whole gang, sitting at picnic tables at the side of Dinky's Outdoor Road Stop Cafe.

"Hey gang, what's up?" you say as you walk over to Velma, Daphne, Fred, Shaggy, and Scooby-Doo.

Shaggy is licking his lips. "Like, I'm so hungry, I could eat a sandwich as big as this table! How about you, Scooby?"

Scooby is sitting next to Shaggy. He nods happily. *"Reah! Reah!"*

"Like, we just got back from another amazing adventure," Shaggy says.

Then he turns to place his order with the waiter. "Like, do you have any sandwiches as big as this table?" Shaggy asks the waiter.

"No, of course not," says the waiter, looking at Shaggy like he's crazy.

"Raw!" Scooby frowns, disappointed.

Shaggy and Scooby place their *regular-size* sandwich order.

Fred turns to smile at you.

"We just got back from the forests of the Pacific Northwest," Fred explains. "So we decided to get the Mystery Machine tuned up after such a long trip."

"It was a pretty exciting mystery we solved. I wish you were there to help us," Daphne tells you. "Would you like to hear about it?"

"You bet!" you say, and you sit down.

"Here you go!" the waiter grunts as he

hands a huge platter of peanut butter and jelly sandwiches to Shaggy and Scooby.

"One hundred and thirty-four peanut butter and jelly sandwiches!" he says.

"Only one hundred and thirty-four?" laughs Velma. "You guys must not be as hungry as usual!"

"Like, these are only appetizers," Shaggy declares.

"Anyway, about our latest mystery," Fred says to you. "I'll bet you could have helped us solve it."

You smile.

You *are* pretty good at solving mysteries.

"Hey, I know!" Daphne smiles. "We'll tell you the story of our latest case, and you can solve it!"

"That sounds like fun!" you laugh.

"I've even got something to help you," Fred says as he holds up a small wire-bound notebook with a purple cover.

Then he hands the notebook over to you. "It's our Clue Keeper for this case, which we call *The Lost Lumberjack*."

"We write down everything that happens in our Clue Keeper," Daphne explains. "The people we meet, the clues we find, and anything we think is important."

"All you have to do is read the Clue Keeper," Velma continues. "We've even added some shortcuts.

"Whenever you see this 👁️ 👁️ , you'll know you've met a suspect in the case. And whenever you see this 🔦 , you've found a clue."

"Our Clue Keeper is divided into sections," Fred says. "At the end of each section, we'll help you organize the things you've found. All you'll need is your own Clue Keeper and a pen or pencil."

"Say, Scoob! Like, where are our manners?" Shaggy asks suddenly, looking at you. "Would you like some of our PB and J, pal?"

"Reah! Reat up!" Scooby says, motioning to the half-eaten sandwiches.

"No, thank you," you answer politely, barely able to stifle a giggle. Scooby's and Shaggy's

faces are covered with peanut butter and jelly. "I'd rather start solving this mystery."

"All right then," Velma says, pointing to the Mystery, Inc. Clue Keeper.

"I wrote up this mystery. Just open it and begin with Clue Keeper Entry Number One of *The Lost Lumberjack*," she says.

And so, you do.

Clue Keeper Entry 1

The Pacific Northwest is beautiful. We drove through the tree-covered mountains of Washington State on our way to visit a historic, century-old sawmill I'd read about. The sawmill attracted a lot of tourists.

"Like, how much farther is this place, Velma?" Shaggy asked me. "Scooby and I are starving! Right, Scoob?"

"Ruh-huh," Scooby whined, trying to look as sad as possible. *"Ry rummy's rumbling!"*

"As a matter of fact, there it is now," Fred

pointed from behind the steering wheel of the Mystery Machine.

Sure enough, up ahead loomed the rustic Pacific Lumber Company sawmill. It was built in 1895 and had supplied a lot of wood to people. Now it had been turned into a tourist attraction. People from all over the country came to see it.

But there was something in front of the sawmill we hadn't expected to see — a group of protesters holding signs, walking in a big circle.

As the Mystery Machine pulled into the mill's parking lot, Scooby and Shaggy immediately jumped out.

"Like, c'mon Scoob!" Shaggy cried happily. "Let's go see if they've got candy bars in the gift shop!"

"Roh, boy! Rhocolate!" Scooby smiled as he hungrily followed.

Fred, Daphne, and I didn't go with Shaggy and Scooby. We wanted to see why the protesters were there. We approached a lady with a bullhorn. She appeared to be the leader.

"Hi, I'm Belinda Picket 👁 👁 ," the lady

with the bullhorn said. "Have you come to join 'The Friends of the Old Mill' in our protest?"

"No, I'm afraid not," Fred answered. "We were just wondering what you were protesting about."

"The old sawmill and the forest around it have been sold to a development company. They want to cut down all the trees and build a town here," Belinda explained. "We're trying to stop it — and we will, too! We've gotten some unexpected help from the ghostly lumberjack!"

"Ghostly lumberjack?" I asked. "Tell us about him. We've had a *little* experience with ghosts."

"People say it's the spooky ghost of a logger who was lost in the woods over fifty years ago and never found. The lumberjack's ghost has been haunting people around here lately," Belinda said. "If a ghost scares people away, then the developers won't want to build a town here. I'm all for that!"

Belinda started to walk away. "If you'll excuse me, I have to get our lunch baskets. Protesting is mighty hungry work."

Belinda smiled and disappeared into the trees. About the same time, Shaggy and Scooby sadly came back from the old sawmill. "Aw man! Like, not only do they *not* have candy bars, they don't even have a gift shop!" Shaggy complained.

We looked for Belinda, to ask if Shaggy and Scooby could join them for lunch, but we couldn't see her anywhere.

Suddenly, we heard a growling from the trees. Out came a strange-looking man in old-fashioned lumberjack clothes — like the kind Paul Bunyan wore. He was over six feet tall and his eyes were completely white . . . and they glowed. It was the ghostly lumberjack!

"*Aaarrrrr!*" the ghost snarled. Then it came lumbering toward us, with arms outstretched and fingers grabbing, grabbing . . . it was grabbing for us!

Velma's Mystery-Solving Tips

"Whew! You can get back to the exciting story after you've made an entry in your Clue Keeper. Did you see the 👀 on page 8? That's your tip that you've found your first suspect. Now answer the questions below about this suspect."

1. What is the suspect's name?

2. Why is she at the old sawmill?

3. How can a scary ghost help her?

Clue Keeper Entry 2

"Zoinks!" cried Shaggy. "Like, run! The ghoulie's got grabby fingers!"

"*Aaaarrr!*" The lumberjack's ghost growled again.

"And it's in a nasty mood," I said. "We'd better back off."

"I think you're right, Velma," Fred said to me. "Once we're clear of him, we can try to figure this mystery out!"

At that moment, one of the protesters saw the ghostly figure. "What's that?" he shouted.

"A ghost," a second protester shrieked.

"Let's get out of here," a third protester cried out. Together, the group fled into the trees, screaming.

The lumberjack's ghost turned toward us. *"Aaaarrrr!"*

"Like, let's scram!" Shaggy yelled, his legs already pumping.

We ran into the old sawmill. Inside were rusty machines, once used to split, shave, and cut logs. These machines had stopped working long ago.

But we didn't have time to enjoy the sights at that moment. The ghost was right on our heels! It snarled and grasped for us angrily. We ran around one of the biggest machines.

"It knows we're in here. We can't run away from it forever," Daphne said.

I saw a little door and yanked it open. There was a small, pitch-dark room on the other side. "Inside, fast," I told my friends. We tumbled in and shut the door. I peeked through the keyhole and watched as the ghoulish ghost passed by, and continued on.

"Jinkies! I think we lost it!" I said.

"Lost what?" asked a deep voice behind us. A bright light snapped on.

We all screamed!

We thought we were alone in the tiny room. But we turned and saw a middle-aged man in a business suit. He was sitting at a desk.

"I'm sorry," the man smiled. "I didn't mean to scare you. I'm K.T. Bricks 👁 👁 , a land developer. This is my office. I shut off the

light so I could catch a quick nap at my desk."

Mr. Bricks was the developer Belinda Picket had told us about. It was his job to arrange for the removal of the sawmill and all the trees around it, so a town could be built there.

"Are you running from something?" Mr. Bricks asked.

"Like, nothing much, man. Just a ghost!" Shaggy said.

"Reah! A rig, rugly rhost!" Scooby added.

Mr. Bricks frowned and ran his hand nervously through his hair. "Oh, no! Not the ghost again!" Mr. Bricks said glumly. "I don't know what to do!"

"Jeepers, what's wrong, Mr. Bricks?" Daphne asked as she sat down in the chair opposite Mr. Bricks. The rest of us crowded around to listen.

"I've been having a terrible time trying to make this land deal work!" Mr. Bricks said. "First it was the protesters. Now this ghost is scaring everybody away. My crews won't work with a ghost around. I'm afraid I might have to call the whole deal off."

"Don't worry, Mr. Bricks," Fred said confidently. "We've solved quite a few mysteries. We'll help you find out what's up with this ghost."

Mr. Bricks looked unsure. "Oh, I wouldn't want you kids to go through any trouble."

"Like, that makes two of us!" Shaggy said. "When it comes to ghosts, that's trouble we don't need!"

"Nonsense," I said. "It's no trouble at all. If you could just show us the different places where the ghost has been spotted, Mr. Bricks, we'll start our investigation."

"Well, if you insist. I'll get my assistant Clay to show you." Mr. Bricks lifted his phone receiver. "Clay likes to camp out in the woods, but he's got a cellular phone," he explained.

In about ten minutes, a large, broad-shouldered man walked into the office. "Hello, Clay," Mr. Bricks said. He introduced us to Clay, who barely smiled.

"Come on, I'll show you where the ghost is usually seen hanging around," Clay said gruffly. He didn't seem like too happy a person.

We thanked Mr. Bricks and followed Clay into the woods. We hadn't gone very far when suddenly, Shaggy and Scooby stuck their noses straight up into the air.

"Like, do you smell what I smell, Scoob, ol' pal?" Shaggy smiled hungrily. "Some-one's been cooking lunch on an open fire!"

"Reah! Reah!" Scooby said excitedly.

Like a shot, Scooby and Shaggy took off, following the pleasant scent of the outdoor barbecue with their noses.

Shaggy and Scooby's
Mystery-Solving Tips

"Like, did you see the 👀 on page 16 and page 19? Then, get your Clue Keeper and answer the questions below about the last entry. Pretty soon, you'll solve this groovy ghost mystery!"

1. Who were the two suspects in the last entry?

2. What are they doing at the old sawmill?

3. How does the ghost affect their plans?

Clue Keeper Entry 3

We followed Shaggy and Scooby through the trees. They had a good lead on us. When it comes to feeding their stomachs, those two can run fast!

"But we're not heading to where the ghost is usually seen!" Clay called grouchily from behind.

I turned back to answer, "Yes, but we don't want to leave our friends alone in the woods. At least, not until we know more about the ghost!"

Clay just shrugged his shoulders and stayed behind.

When I finally reached a clearing where the gang had stopped, Shaggy and Scooby were circling a pit dug into the sand. Someone had built a barbecue there and had been recently cooking food.

"Whoever was chowing down here, has eaten and run," Shaggy said.

"Well, maybe it's not a total loss," I said. "Let's look around the area for some more clues."

We searched the clearing. Whoever had been cooking there had been very tidy. No trash was left behind.

"I found something over here," Fred pointed to a scrap of material hanging on a branch . "Maybe it's from the ghost's disguise," he whispered. "It looks like the same material, anyway."

"Like, if it *is* a disguise, Fred," Shaggy said. "I don't know about you guys, but that spook looked pretty real to me."

"Ree, roo!" Scooby nodded.

"Don't be silly. You two know there's no such thing as ghosts," I said. "There has to be a logical explanation."

"Yeah," agreed Fred. "Why would a ghost cook food?"

"Like, maybe it was *frightfully* hungry!" Shaggy joked, then laughed.

Scooby joined in, *"Ree-hee-hee!"*

"Verrrry funny, you two," I said sarcasti-

cally. "But if you ever want to solve this mystery so we can leave and get lunch, you'd better start looking for more clues!"

"Zoinks! That's right!" Shaggy gulped. "We still haven't had lunch! C'mon, Scoob let's get to detecting!"

But Scooby already had his nose to the ground and was quickly sniffing all around. *"Sniff! Sniff! Sniff!"*

"Hey, gang! I think I found another clue over here!" Daphne called from over by a big pine tree. She was walking around the base of the huge tree. It was so big, Daphne disappeared behind it.

"Wait for us, Daph!" Fred called. "We don't want to lose anyone."

As Fred, Shaggy, Scooby, and I approached, we heard Daphne say, "It's around here on the other side! Come look, it's . . ."

Then Daphne screamed, *"Eeeeeeeeeeeeee!"*

We ran to the other side of the tree. Fred shouted, "Daphne, are you okay? Daphne?"

But Daphne wasn't there.

"She just disappeared into thin air," I gasped.

"Or, like, maybe the ghost got her!" Shaggy said with his eyes open wide.

"*Rooh-oooh-ooh!*" said Scooby dizzily, and then he fainted onto the ground.

"Boy, I sure was worried about danger-prone Daphne. I'm sure you'd like to know what happened to her, too. But before we continue the story, jot down some of the clues found in the last entry. You did see the [flashlight], didn't you, on page 22? Great! Grab your Clue Keeper and answer the questions below."

1. What were the clues found in the last entry?

2. What do you think these clues have to do with the ghost?

3. Could any of the suspects have left the clues? Which suspects?

Clue Keeper Entry 4

"Where did Daphne go?" I wondered.

Fred pointed to the base of the tree. "Look, some kind of secret door!"

Sure enough, there was a small door on the ground beside the big tree. It looked as if you would fall through if you stood on it.

Then I heard a groan. Daphne was on the ground, behind a nearby rock. "I tripped over that door," she said.

Daphne got to her feet. Then she smiled

up at us. "Well, what are you waiting for? I've discovered a secret passageway."

Fred and Daphne climbed down carefully. I walked back around the wide pine tree to get the others.

Shaggy was fanning Scooby, who looked like he was still passed out.

"Zoinks! Like, poor, ol' Scooby-Doo has fainted due to excess terror and hunger! We need one dozen extra-thick pizzas here, stat!"

"*Rith anchovies,*" Scooby whispered, opening one eye just a little.

"Come on, you fakers," I said. "Unless you *want* to stay out here alone in the forest where the ghost is."

That got Scooby and Shaggy moving. They were up and running so fast, they passed by me. But they waited outside the open secret trapdoor, gazing into it nervously.

"Down you go," I told them.

"Like, no way Velma," Shaggy said. "That ghost is *way* too creepy!"

"*Reah, really reepy!*" Scooby agreed.

"Get going," I insisted. "Unless you want

to meet the ghost in the woods." I climbed in. Shaggy and Scooby came down after me.

Fred and Daphne were waiting for us at the bottom of the rickety ladder. We looked around. There were lights mounted on the wall every few hundred feet. It was quite easy to find our way around.

"I wonder if the ghost uses this tunnel?" Fred said.

"We'll find out if we run into him down here," said Daphne.

"Zoinks! I hope not!" Shaggy cried. "Scoob and I came down into this tunnel to avoid the ghastly ghoulie, not to run into him!"

Everyone stepped quietly through the tunnel. At every turn we expected the lumberjack to pop out, with his weird glowing eyes.

After a while, the tunnel came to an end at a locked door.

"Like, not a problem," smiled Shaggy. "Not when one of the greatest lock-pickers in the world is your best friend. Take it away, Scooby!"

Scooby proudly stepped up to the locked door. He looked at the lock. *"Riece of rake!"* he grinned confidently.

Scooby lifted his tail and put the tip of it to the lock. He concentrated. Suddenly, the tip of Scooby's tail turned into a key shape. He slipped it into the lock.

Click!

Scooby opened the door, stood up on his hind legs, and elegantly ushered us through the door.

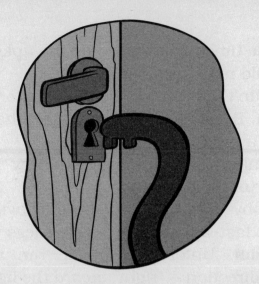

"*Rafter you, radies and rentlemen!*" Scooby said, then he laughed. "*Ree hee hee!*"

We were all surprised when we saw what was on the other side — the old sawmill! But it was a part of the sawmill we hadn't seen before. There were all sorts of old lumber-making machines, but they weren't rusty. In fact, they looked like they still worked.

There was a giant circular saw, a log splitter, and even a machine that banded bundles of logs together with thick metal bands.

"Jinkies!" I said. "I wonder who would

take the time to clean and do the upkeep on these old machines? And why?"

I didn't have time to wonder for long, though. Because suddenly, in the shadows, moved a mysterious figure.

"Zoinks! It's the ghost!" Shaggy yelled. "Like, run for it, Scoob!"

Scooby didn't have to be told twice. He ran as fast as his Great Dane legs would take him. Unfortunately, he ran in the wrong direction — right *toward* the figure in the shadows!

Daphne's Mystery-Solving Tips

"Jeepers! Things were pretty exciting for Scooby! We'll get back to the story in a minute. But first, did you see the ▬▬● on page 27? That could be an important clue. Open your Clue Keeper and answer the questions below."

1. What clue did you find in this entry?

2. What do you think the ghost might have used this clue for?

3. Which of the suspects may have known about this clue?

33

Clue Keeper Entry 5

The mysterious visitor was over six feet tall. Scooby ran right into him, was smashed flat, and fell prone onto the floor.

Shaggy looked at me. "Zoinks! Velma, the ghost got Scooby-Doo!"

"That's no ghost, Shaggy," I said.

Sure enough, a man — not a ghost — sat up. He was wearing a pair of oily overalls and looked to be around seventy years old. He pulled out a pair of false teeth and stuck them into his mouth.

"Naw, I ain't no ghost," the man declared,

adjusting the teeth. "I'm Cyrus Tinker 👁 👁 , and I've been working at this sawmill for over fifty-five years."

Mr. Tinker told us that he was still employed by the sawmill as a handyman. It was his job to keep the place open for tourists.

"Fixing these machines is sort of a hobby. I do it in my spare time," Mr. Tinker said. "I'm sure going to hate seeing them tear this ol' place down."

We told Mr. Tinker that we were looking for the ghost, how we had followed clues to the tunnel, and how the tunnel had led to the door.

"You won't find a ghost down there," Mr. Tinker said. "Ain't nobody has used that old tunnel or gone through that door in years. Even I don't. I come in through a door in the sawmill. In fact, the only other person I know of that's got a key to the trapdoor is that land developer feller, Mr. Bricks."

"Well, somebody's been using it," I said. "It's open and there are lights on."

"I ain't got time to worry about it, young lady," Mr. Tinker said, wiping his hands with

a cloth that was just as dirty as his hands were. "Good luck with your ghost hunting."

Mr. Tinker ambled away, mumbling under his breath about "crazy kids."

"I think we should ask Mr. Bricks about the tunnel," suggested Fred.

We went back to Mr. Bricks's office. Fred knocked on the door.

"Mr. Bricks?" Fred called.

Fred put his hand on the door handle and slowly turned it. It wasn't locked. After taking a deep breath, Fred inched the door open.

Creeeeeeak!

We stepped over the threshold and into Mr. Bricks's office. Then we stopped and stood petrified.

We found ourselves face-to-face with the lumberjack's ghost!

We backed away quietly.

The lumberjack's ghost stepped into the room. It was dark and we didn't know if he saw us. But then he raised his arms and growled. His eyes glowed! He saw us!

There was only one way to escape. And that was to run right past him!

"Jinkies! That was pretty scary, let me tell you. I remember wishing I'd left my glasses behind, so I couldn't see that growling ghoul! And speaking of seeing, did you see the 👀 on page 35? Terrific! Now, take your Clue Keeper and write down your answers to the questions below."

1. Who is the suspect you discovered in this entry?

2. How would this suspect benefit if the ghost scared everyone away?

3. Could this suspect have left the clues in the earlier chapters?

Clue Keeper Entry 6

"*Rhost!*" Scooby cried.

"Zoinks!" Shaggy yelled.

"Jeepers!" Daphne hollered.

"Jinkies!" I gulped.

"Run for it!" Fred suggested. And we did.

The ghost chased us upstairs and downstairs in the old mill. We ran into doors and out of other doors. We hid behind the machines and under desks. But the ghost of the lumberjack still found us.

One of the things that still worked in the old sawmill was a long network of water troughs. These were used by the loggers in the old days to move logs from here to there. They actually floated the heavy logs. The owner of the sawmill kept the water flowing through the old troughs for the tourists' sake. It looked pretty cool.

We tried swimming away from the creepy lumberjack through the troughs. But the ghost cut us off, and we had to run again.

Finally, we ran back outside and away from the sawmill. After going a short way, we realized we'd gone the *wrong* way. Just up ahead, we could see that the forest ended at a cliff.

"Great! Now what are we going to do?" Fred asked.

We ran to the edge of the cliff. We could see a winding river far below.

We were trapped, and the lumberjack's ghost was right behind us.

"*Aaarrrr!*"

"Like, good-bye Scoob, ol' pal!" Shaggy tearfully hugged Scooby-Doo. "It's been nice knowing you!"

"*Roh, nooooo!*" Scooby sobbed. He blew his runny nose on Shaggy's shirt. "*Honk!*"

Then I spotted something that might save us. "Come on, this way!" I called and the gang ran with me along the edge of the cliff.

"Where are we going, Velma?" Daphne asked me.

"There!" I said, and I pointed.

We were next to a big water trough that had been built from the old mill to the cliff. The trough led over the cliff, and then tilted downward at a very steep angle. Water was rushing through the trough and down to the river a mile below.

"Jump!" I said.

We didn't have any choice. The ghost was right behind us. It reached out with its gnarled hands and was just about to grab Daphne.

We jumped.

Down, down, down we slid! We went faster and faster until the rushing water was a roar in our ears. It was kind of scary . . . but it was kind of fun, too!

"Wheeeee!" I hollered. I couldn't help myself. It was like a roller coaster.

Fred looked back up the trough. "We're in luck! The lumberjack isn't coming after us!"

"Like, pardon me if I don't *feel* that lucky, Fred," Shaggy cried. "I've got the feeling our spirits are about to drop! Look!"

Shaggy was right. The trough suddenly ended up ahead, and the water dumped about fifty feet to the river below. Very soon we would be dumped, too!

Scooby covered his eyes. *"Rye can't rook!"* he gulped.

The trough ended and then we were falling, falling, falling. . . .

Clue Keeper Entry 7

Then, *splash*!

We all struggled, swimming up to the surface. When we broke water, we all took deep breaths . . . we made it! We quickly swam to the edge of the river to get out of the cold mountain water.

"Well, we're soaked to the skin, but at least that supernatural spook didn't get us!" smiled Daphne. "Now what?"

"Now back to the sawmill to figure a way to trap that ghost!" Fred replied. "Let's go, gang."

"Zoinks! Like, no way are we going to be able to make it, Fred," Shaggy said. "We haven't eaten since breakfast and don't have the energy."

"Would you be able to make it if I gave you some Scooby Snacks?" I said, pulling out a handful of snacks from my pocket. "So, is it a deal?"

"Reah! Reah!" Scooby jumped up and down.

"They're kind of wet, but . . ." I started to say.

But it didn't matter. Shaggy and Scooby took the soggy treats out of my hands and gobbled them down in an instant.

Just then, a truck drove up the road near where we stood. It was driven by Mr. Bricks. His assistant Clay was in the passenger seat.

"Do you kids need a ride up to the sawmill?" Mr. Bricks asked as the truck pulled to a stop. Clay frowned at us.

We all piled into the back of the truck, and Mr. Bricks drove on. Fred asked Mr. Bricks about the secret tunnel, but the developer said he'd never been inside. He said he'd lost the key to the door several weeks earlier.

There were all sorts of interesting things in the back of the truck — charts, maps, and surveying equipment. But there was one thing that seemed out of place.

"Look at this," I said quietly as I pointed to a box in the corner. "It's a stage actor's makeup box ." I opened the box. There were all sorts of makeup — blushes, rouge, and greasepaint. "Now, why would a developer and his assistant need one of these?" I wondered out loud.

By this time, the truck had made it back to the old sawmill.

"We're here," Mr. Bricks turned to us in the back. "And I'm happy to say all the protesters are gone! I guess you kids will be leaving now, right?"

"No, sir," Fred answered. "Not until we solve this mystery."

We climbed out of the truck and saw that Mr. Bricks was only partly right. Not *all* the protesters had left.

Belinda Picket was still there.

"Are you giving up your protest?" Fred asked Belinda as Mr. Bricks and Clay walked back up to the sawmill.

"No way!" Belinda smiled. "I'm just going back to town to get some new protesters to help me. This time I'll try to find ones that won't be scared by phantoms so easily!"

She got in her car, waved good-bye, and drove away.

"All right, gang, let's get busy," Fred said. "Time to catch a ghost!"

"Like, did you notice the far-out  on page 47? Outta sight, man! It's a really important clue! Make sure you answer all the questions below in your Clue Keeper."

1. What was the clue you discovered in this entry?

2. What do you think this clue is used for?

3. Which of the suspects do you think uses this clue?

49

Clue Keeper Entry 8

"I'm pretty sure I know who the lumberjack really is," I said. "But we'll have to catch the culprit in the act. Here's the plan: Shaggy and Scooby will hike around the woods until the ghost comes after them. Once it starts chasing you, lead it over to the trapdoor by the big tree. We'll open it and cover up the opening with some thin branches.With a little luck, the lumberjack will fall through the trapdoor into the secret passageway."

"Fred and I will be waiting in the tunnel with this net," Daphne said. She held up a net we keep in the back of the Mystery Machine for emergencies just like this. "Then we'll catch it!"

"I'll act as lookout," I said. "I'll hide by the tree and let Fred and Daphne know when you boys and the creepy ghost are getting close."

"Let's do it!" Fred smiled.

"Like, no way!" Shaggy said suddenly. "Why do Scoob and I always have to attract the grisly ghoulies? Do we look like bait or something?"

"Well . . ." Daphne started.

But I pulled out a handful of soggy Scooby Snacks. Shaggy and Scooby immediately agreed to lure the ghost in exchange for the treats.

Soon we were in our places: Fred and Daphne under the trapdoor with the net, me behind the tree, and Shaggy and Scooby romping through the woods.

Shaggy was yelling, "I sure hope a scary *ghost* doesn't come out of the woods and eat me."

"Ree, neither!" Scooby shouted. *"A rhost*

rith rig, rharp reeth!" Scooby pulled back his lips and bared his fangs horribly.

"Uh, like, Scoob, let's not overdo it, okay?" Shaggy said. "You're kind of creeping me out."

"Rorry, Raggy."

A few minutes passed . . . and then we heard it.

"Aaarrrr!"

The lumberjack's ghost appeared through

the trees and headed right at Shaggy and Scooby. They ran like the wind. The lumberjack's ghost chased them.

I watched as Scooby and Shaggy led it to the tree where I was waiting.

"Here they come!" I called to Daphne and Fred under the trapdoor.

Shaggy was in the lead, then came Scooby. They ran past where I was hidden. The ghost ran up to the trapdoor.

It lifted its foot over it, it brought its foot down . . .

. . . and it stepped right over the trap-door, and kept going.

"Zoinks!" Shaggy cried. "Now what?"

"Keep running," I yelled.

Shaggy and Scooby ran toward the saw-mill, with the ghost right behind. Daphne and Fred climbed out of the tunnel, and we followed as fast as we could.

In the sawmill, we found them near the machines that Cyrus had rebuilt. The ghoul was chasing Shaggy and Scooby around the log splitter. The lumberjack was gaining on them, so they leaped up on the huge circular saw platform.

"Rurrrrrrrrrrr!" Suddenly, the saw was going round and round! The moving belt was edging Scooby and Shaggy right into the sharp blades! I looked at the nearby control panel and saw that it was the ghost who had turned the saw on.

"Run, you guys!" Daphne shouted. "Get away from that saw!"

"Like, yikes!" cried Shaggy. He and

Scooby jumped off the circular saw just in time, and ran right past the ghost.

The ghost lunged for them, but missed and lost its balance. It fell onto the banding machine platform. Fred immediately turned the machine on. Quick as a wink, the ghastly ghost of the lumberjack was bound up by several sturdy metal bands.

"Yay! We got it!" Daphne cheered.

"Yes, and let's just see who *it* is!" I said as I pulled off the ghost's mask.

Scooby and Shaggy were biting into another platter of peanut butter and jelly sandwiches as you look up from the gang's detective journal.

"Well, now you've met all the suspects and found all the clues," Fred says. "Do you think you can solve the mystery?"

You smile and say you think you can.

"Terrific!" Daphne says. "Here's some advice — look at your list of suspects and clues, then answer these questions."

"First, who do you think had a good reason to scare people away from the sawmill?" Velma asks.

"Second, who do you think had the know-how to scare people away from the sawmill?" Fred asks.

"Third, who do you think had the opportunity to scare people away from the sawmill?" Daphne asks.

"See if you can eliminate any of the suspects first," Velma suggests. "Then using all of the information you've collected, as well as your own smarts, try to figure who the lumberjack's ghost really is."

Jinkies! It's time for you to guess whodunnit! Do you think you know who it is? When you're ready, look at the next page and discover the ending of The Case of the Lost Lumberjack.

"**M**r. Bricks and his assistant Clay were behind the whole lumberjack's ghost mystery," Velma explains. "Clay would dress up like the ghoul to frighten away tourists and protesters. Once they were gone, the ghost would have stopped making appearances."

"You know that our other two suspects were Belinda Picket, the protester and Cyrus Tinker, the handyman," Daphne adds.

"But Belinda wouldn't want to scare anyone away, especially protesters," Velma comments.

"Cyrus Tinker seemed too proud of the old mill to want to keep tourists away," Fred says. "Plus he had false teeth, and whoever was masquerading as the ghost was cooking meat in the forest — meat that a person with false teeth couldn't eat."

"But we knew Clay liked to camp outside. Mr. Bricks told us," Velma continues. "He was the likely one to build a barbecue pit in the woods. And the scrap of material hanging on a branch near the barbecue pit matched the ghost's clothing perfectly."

"What clinched it for us was the makeup case in the back of Mr. Bricks's truck." Fred smiles. "It had everything Clay would need to make himself up to look like a scary ghost."

"Once the protesters and tourists were gone, the ghost would become a distant memory. After a while, the workers would forget about the ghost and start tearing down the sawmill and cutting down the trees," Velma concludes. "Soon enough, there would have been a new town where the sawmill stands."

All the Mystery, Inc. gang are now looking at you.

"So, how did you do?" Daphne asks.

"I'll bet you solved the mystery like a pro!" Velma smiles. "You're pretty smart."

"I'll tell you what was *really* smart — when they declared the old sawmill a historical monument," Fred says. "Now it will never be torn down."

"Like, even smarter was when old Cyrus added a gift shop," Shaggy grinned. "A gift shop with lots and lots of candy bars!"

"Rummmm! Rhocolate!" nods Scooby.

You get up to go.

"Come back and visit us again," Velma says. "There are always plenty of mysteries that need solving."

"And, like, always plenty of peanut butter and jelly sandwiches to munch!" Shaggy says. "Right, Scoob, ol' pal?"

"Rooby-Rooby-Doo!" Scooby cheers in full agreement.